See Otto

See Otto

story and pictures by
D AVID M ILGRIM

Atheneum Books for Young Readers
New York London Toronto Sydney Singapore

Atheneum Books for Young Readers
An imprint of Simon & Schuster Children's Publishing Division
1230 Avenue of the Americas
New York, New York 10020

The text of this book is set in Meta.
The illustrations are rendered in digital pen-and-ink.
Printed in the United States of America
First Edition

2 4 6 8 10 9 7 5 3 1

Library of Congress Cataloging-in-Publication Data
Milgrim, David.
See Otto / by David Milgrim.—1st ed.
p.   cm.
Summary: Otto the robot lands on Earth, where he is chased by a
rhinoceros and befriended by some monkeys.
ISBN 0-689-84416-6
[1. Robots—Fiction. 2. Rhinoceroses—Fiction. 3. Monkeys—Fiction.]
I. Title.
PZ7.M59485 Se 2002
[E]—dc21   2001046369

See Otto

story and pictures by
D AVID M ILGRIM

Atheneum Books for Young Readers
New York London Toronto Sydney Singapore

Atheneum Books for Young Readers
An imprint of Simon & Schuster Children's Publishing Division
1230 Avenue of the Americas
New York, New York 10020

Ready-to-Read is a registered trademark of Simon & Schuster, Inc.

The text of this book is set in Meta.
The illustrations are rendered in digital pen-and-ink.
Printed in the United States of America
First Edition

2 4 6 8 10 9 7 5 3 1

Library of Congress Cataloging-in-Publication Data
Milgrim, David.
See Otto / by David Milgrim.—1st ed.
p.   cm.
Summary: Otto the robot lands on Earth, where he is chased by a
rhinoceros and befriended by some monkeys.
ISBN 0-689-84416-6
[1. Robots—Fiction. 2. Rhinoceroses—Fiction. 3. Monkeys—Fiction.]
I. Title.
PZ7.M59485 Se 2002
[E]—dc21   2001046369

See Otto.

See Otto go.

Go,
Otto,
go!

Go, go, go.

Look, Otto is out of gas.

See Otto fall.

Fall,
fall,
fall.

See Otto smile.

Smile, Otto, smile.

See
Otto
run.

See Otto fly.

Bye, Otto, bye.

See Flip.
See Flip paint.

See Flop.
See Flop sit.

Look, here comes Otto!

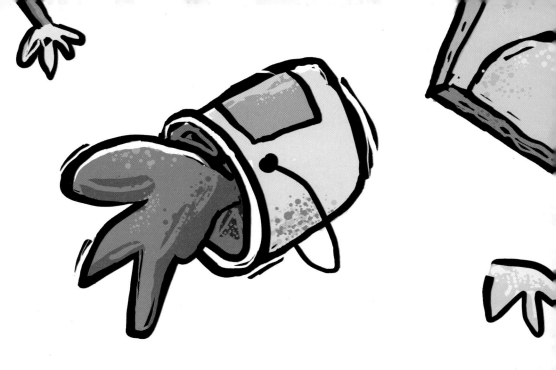

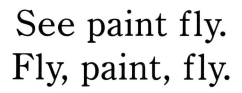

See paint fly.
Fly, paint, fly.

See everyone laugh.

Laugh, everyone, laugh.